Emily and Alice
Best Friends

Written by
Joyce Champion

Illustrated by
Suçie Stevenson

Gulliver Books • Harcourt, Inc.
San Diego   New York   London

D1110315

Text copyright © 1993 by Joyce Champion
Illustrations copyright © 1993 by Suçie Stevenson

All rights reserved. No part of this publication may be reproduced
or transmitted in any form or by any means, electronic or mechanical, including
photocopy, recording, or any information storage and retrieval system
without permission in writing from the publisher.

Requests for permission to make copies of any part of the work
should be mailed to: Permissions Department, Harcourt, Inc.,
6277 Sea Harbor Drive, Orlando, Florida 32887–6777.

www.harcourt.com

First published 1993 as *Emily and Alice*
First Gulliver Books paperback edition 2001

Gulliver Books is a trademark of Harcourt, Inc.,
registered in the United States of America and other jurisdictions.

Library of Congress Cataloging-in-Publication Data
Champion, Joyce.
Emily and Alice, best friends/Joyce Champion; [illustrated by] Suçie Stevenson.
p. cm.
"Gulliver Books."
Summary: When Alice moves in next door to Emily, the girls quickly become
best friends even as they learn that they sometimes must do what the other wants.
[1. Best friends—Fiction.] I. Stevenson, Suçie, ill. II. Title.
PZ8.C3585Er 2001
[E]—dc21 99-6209
ISBN 0-15-202198-1

A C E G H F D B

The illustrations in this book were done in
acrylic and indelible felt-tip pen on Bristol Vellum.
The display type was set in Remedy Double and Caxton Bold.
The text type was set in Perpetua.
Printed and bound by Tien Wah Press, Singapore
This book was printed on totally chlorine-free Nymolla Matte Art paper.
Production supervision by Sandra Grebenar and Pascha Gerlinger
Designed by Trina Stahl and Lori McThomas Buley

For Lindsay,
who has straight blond hair and loves
all kinds of cookies
—J. C.

For Emily Stevenson
—S. S.

Best Friends

Emily looked out the window and jumped up and down. "Yippeee!" she shouted. "New neighbors! There's a girl with long black hair and pink sandals. I like her already."

Emily ran to the front door. "Where are you going?" her mother called.

"Next door," answered Emily. "I'm inviting the new girl over for peanut butter cookies and milk."

As she ran across the yard, Emily suddenly thought, *Oh no. Maybe the new girl doesn't even like peanut butter cookies. Maybe she'd rather have graham crackers.*

Emily started walking slowly. *Maybe the new girl doesn't want a friend with red ponytails and striped kneesocks. Maybe she only likes long hair and sandals.*

Emily stopped walking. *I'm going home.*

Just then the new girl turned around. "Hi," she called. "I'm Alice. What's your name?"

"Emily," Emily told her. "Do you like peanut butter cookies?"

"I *love* peanut butter cookies," said Alice.

Emily smiled. "Then come to my house," she said. "We've got lots of them."

Emily and Alice skipped across the yard.
"I like your long hair, Alice," said Emily, as they
skipped along.

"I like your striped kneesocks," said Alice.

When they got to the house, Emily let Alice
try on her striped kneesocks.

Alice let Emily braid her long hair.

They both ate lots of peanut butter cookies, laughed at each other's milk mustaches, and decided to be best friends.

Baby Sam

Emily skated over to Alice's house. "Alice, Alice!" she called. "Come on out. We have to practice our skating."

"I can't come out today!" shouted Alice. "Baby Sam is sick. You come in."

Emily pulled off her skates. She ran upstairs to Alice's room. "Alice," she said, "you don't have a baby brother or a baby sister. So who is Baby Sam?"

"Grandma gave me Baby Sam for my birthday," said Alice. "Come and see how sick he is."

Emily looked hard at Baby Sam. "He doesn't look sick to me," she said. "Let's go skating."

"Baby Sam is *very* sick," insisted Alice. "He already has a high fever and soon he'll break out in spots. I can't leave him now."

"But, Alice," said Emily, "look outside. The sun is shining. The sky is so blue. We've got to go skating."

"I can't go," said Alice. "Baby Sam needs me."

Emily thought for a moment. Then she smiled. "You're very lucky that I'm here," she told Alice.

Emily went into the bathroom. She came back with a cup of water. "*I* am the doctor," she announced. "And this is special medicine. It will make Baby Sam better in no time. Now let's go skating."

"*Oops,*" said Alice. "Baby Sam just spilled his special medicine. Now he's crying."

Emily ran down to the kitchen. She hurried back with paper towels. "There, the medicine is all cleaned up. Now can we skate?"

"Not yet," said Alice. "First Baby Sam wants you to sing him to sleep."

Emily sighed and sat down on Alice's bed.

She sang: "*Go to sleep. It is late. If you don't, we can't skate.*"

"Shhh," Alice whispered. "Baby Sam is sleeping. Now we can skate."

Emily and Alice tiptoed out of the bedroom.

"Now I am almost too tired to skate," said Emily.

"Me, too," said Alice. "It's not easy being a baby-sitter."

"Sometimes," said Emily, "it's not easy being a best friend, either."

Stormy Day

Emily stared out the window. "What a ter-rible day," she said. "This rain will never stop." She picked up the phone and dialed Alice's number.

"Alice," she said, "come over to my house and we'll think of something to do."

"It's raining too hard," Alice answered. "I don't want to get wet. You come here."

Emily frowned at the phone. "Alice," she said, "I asked you first. Besides, if I go over there *I'll* get wet."

"If you were really my friend," yelled Alice, "you would come over!"

"If you were *my* friend," shouted Emily, "you would come here!"

Alice hung up on Emily. Emily slammed down the phone. "Who needs that Alice anyway," she grumbled.

Emily put on her roller skates. She skated in circles around her room.

But it wasn't much fun skating inside. And it wasn't any fun skating without Alice.

At lunchtime, Emily had a picnic with jam sandwiches and a pitcher of lemonade. But a picnic wasn't the same inside. And a picnic wasn't any good without Alice.

After lunch, Emily pressed her nose against the window. *Maybe Alice won't want me for a friend anymore*, she thought. *Maybe Alice will invite a new friend over to play.*

Emily twisted her ponytails. *Probably Alice called the Tupper twins. And maybe even Chuckie Jones. I bet she invited the whole neighborhood!*

Emily grabbed her jacket and ran out into the rain. There was Alice crossing the yard.

"Alice!" she called. "What are you doing out here?"

"Going to your house," answered Alice.

"But I'm going to *your* house," said Emily.

Emily and Alice looked at each other.

"Come on. Let's go to your house," said Alice.

"No," said Emily. "Let's go to yours."

Alice started to yell. Emily almost started to shout. But then Emily looked at Alice and smiled instead.

"Alice," Emily said, "you have a rainy head."

"You have a drippy nose," said Alice.

They looked at each other all wet and dripping, and started to laugh.

"Hey," said Alice, "getting wet is fun."

"That's only because we're getting wet together," Emily told her.

Alice pointed to a giant puddle. "I know what will be even more fun," she said. "Let's get soaked *together*!"